Shopping
for Lunch

by Susan Blackaby
illustrated by James Demski Jr.

Special thanks to our advisers for their expertise:

Adria F. Klein, Ph.D.
Professor Emeritus, California State University
San Bernardino, California

Susan Kesselring, M.A.
Literacy Educator
Rosemount–Apple Valley–Eagan (Minnesota) School District

PiCTURE WiNDOW BOOKS
Minneapolis, Minnesota

Mom and Joe go to the grocery store.

4

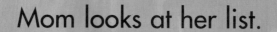

Mom looks at her list.

- APPLES
- BREAD
- PEANUT BUTTER
- JELLY
- MILK

6

Joe gets a cart.

They get red apples.

They get wheat bread.

They get peanut butter and strawberry jelly.

They get chocolate milk.

Mom and Joe pay for the food.
They load the car and go home.

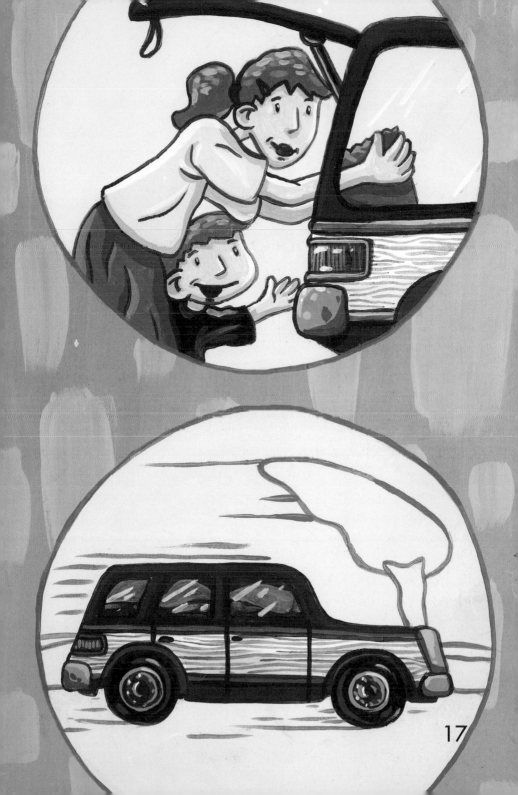

The clock says noon.

It's time for lunch.

What will Mom and Joe have for lunch?

They'll have everything they bought
at the grocery store.

More *Read-it!* Readers

Bright pictures and fun stories help you practice your reading skills. Look for more books at your level.

Ann Plants a Garden 1-4048-1010-2
The Babysitter 1-4048-1187-7
Bess and Tess 1-4048-1013-7
The Best Soccer Player 1-4048-1055-2
Dan Gets Set 1-4048-1011-0
Fishing Trip 1-4048-1004-8
Jen Plays 1-4048-1008-0
Joey's First Day 1-4048-1174-5
Just Try It 1-4048-1175-3
Mary's Art 1-4048-1056-0
The Missing Tooth 1-4048-1592-9
Moving Day 1-4048-1006-4
Pat Picks Up 1-4048-1059-5
A Place for Mike 1-4048-1012-9
Room to Share 1-4048-1185-0
Syd's Room 1-4048-1585-6
Wes Gets a Pet 1-4048-1060-9
Winter Fun for Kat 1-4048-1007-2
A Year of Fun 1-4048-1009-9

Looking for a specific title or level? A complete list of *Read-it!* Readers is available on our Web site:

www.picturewindowbooks.com